CONTENTS

CHAPTER 1

Welcome to Trashland

If your phone goes wrong, do you throw it away? How about your TV or your tablet or your speakers? Or do you recycle these things?

I bet you recycle. You're told it's the right thing to do. It's kinder to the earth, right?

Sure it is.

It's funny, the way the world works. Companies spend millions making cool electronic stuff like smartphones. The bits inside have to be exact, or they won't work.

People working on factory production lines carefully put the whole thing together so it's perfect: sleek and shiny and brand new. You buy it. You love it.

But when the thing is old or stops working, it's not sent *back* to the factory. There's no production line waiting to take it apart again and rescue the bits inside that still work, or take out the precious metals so they can be used again. Getting rid of this thing is not the company's problem. They made it real good, and you bought it. It's yours. If it doesn't work any more, it's your problem.

So you take it to the dump and you go home and it stops being your problem.

Instead, it becomes ours.

*

I like it best here at night cos you can't see so much. There are small fires blazing in the dump 24/7, but I'm in a tiny shack with a sheet over it, which keeps out some of the smoke.

I guess I'm lucky cos I have a sack for a pillow and some cardboard to lie on. Thing is, I share the shack with five chickens and they are noisy. I guard them for this guy during the night so he lets me stay in the shack for free. Unless something happens to one of the chickens, then I pay plenty. I've still got bruises from the last time a chicken got out and a dog killed it, and that was almost a month ago now.

I have a headache too, but that's the bad air. The smoke fills you up and makes you sick.

I dream of living in a proper house. When I look out through the holes in the sheet, I can see dark shadows behind the fires. They could almost be buildings, you know? Buildings with no lights at the windows. A shut-up city, all empty.

But they're not buildings.

The sun rises, big like an orange spilling bright juice between the clouds, and I wake up coughing. The sunlight shows you what the firelight can't: there are no real buildings out there behind the smoke. There are just piles of trash. Stacks of fridge-freezers and dishwashers piled up high. Mountains of TVs and hard drives. Teetering towers of tyres waiting to be burned. The waste stretches out as far as I can see.

I'm Theo. I'm thirteen, I think. I've been stuck here in the mega-dump for more than a year. Living. Working. Watching the chickens.

Waiting.

Dad brought me here and then he left. He said he was coming back. He was waving to me and he definitely said it.

I guess something happened.

Stuff *does* happen, doesn't it? And some of it's crazy.

Like, I bet you never thought that useless DVD player you threw out could end up all the way over here in Ghana, huh? Or that old Xbox 360. Or that crappy mobile your friends made fun of.

Well, chances are it did end up here. From Europe and America, all the way here to West Africa. I hope you're listening, cos this stuff is true. Mr Ghazi told me, and he knows lots cos he runs things here in the dump.

Mr Ghazi's my boss. He organises us child workers. It's not easy, cos there are hundreds of us kids here. And thousands more who are older. And we're all scrabbling about in the dirt and the muck for the tatty treasures that can bring us the cash we need to eat each day.

Mr Ghazi says we're heroes. We're the ones who are really saving the planet.

See, if you bury electronic trash it doesn't rot away. It stays where it is and makes the soil bad. No country wants to bury that stuff in their own soil, but there are laws to stop people sending away their trash to other countries.

Some of the recycling companies get around that by not calling it trash. They call it "used electronics" instead and load up big boats full of it. Some of it ends up in Accra, the capital of Ghana. Some of it can be fixed and sold on. Some of it can't.

If it can't, then it gets dumped here in Agbogbloshie. That's a big name, but you don't have to worry about how to say it.

I call it home, but you can just call it Trashland.

CHAPTER 2

Fighting Strangers

Did you ever wake up and find yourself face to face with a stranger? That's what happened to me this one day.

My eyes flick open and there's some random kid bending over me. And so I shout and I push him back. The chickens go crazy clucking beside me. This boy tries to run, but he slips on an old melon rind. He falls through the sheet and into the mud outside.

That's when I see he's got my magnet in his hand. He must've come here to steal it.

No way I'm letting him do that. For me, no magnet means no work.

I spend my days waving that magnet over the ground to find scraps of metal left behind by the older guys. Nails, screws, paperclips, bolts – on their own they're worth nothing, but if I can get enough of them each day, they'll keep me alive.

I put the scraps I find in my sack and take them to Mr Ghazi, who weighs the metal and gives me money for it. There are a hundred other kids doing the same thing, but I'm faster than most. Maybe I'm just hungrier than they are.

Anyway, I throw myself on top of the kid before he can run away with my magnet. "Give it back!" I shout at him.

He won't let go. He's strong, but I twist the magnet out of his grip and roll away, swearing. "Get out of here," I say.

The boy sits up and holds up his hands like he's saying, *Be chill*. "I wasn't gonna take your magnet," he tells me. "I was just checking it out."

"Liar."

"I wanted to see how well it works," the boy says. "I need help, see?"

The boy is looking at me. His face is trying to be friendly, but his eyes don't smile. I don't trust him.

"My name's Emanuel," he says. "What's yours?"

"Theo." I hold up the magnet. I scratched my name into it when I got it. "See?"

Emanuel gets up. He's taller than me but even skinnier. "You can write," he says. "Can you read too?"

"Get lost," I reply.

"I *am* lost." Emanuel shrugs. "I turned up here yesterday."

I notice then that his hands and his clothes are pretty clean. He must be telling the truth about being new around here.

"I'm here on business," Emanuel goes on. He nods slowly, like he's the man.

"What business?" I ask.

He doesn't answer me. "I saw you work for hours yesterday, Theo. You pick up more than the others. I could use your help with this … business."

"Yeah, well, *Emanuel*," I snort. I don't have time for this guy and his games. "I have my own stuff to do."

"Help me and you could earn proper money," says Emanuel.

"Sure I could," I say, and cross to the big oil can of rainwater beside the chickens. I gulp some down and gasp. It tastes horrible from all the smoke and dirt around here. I dish some out for the chickens. Sometimes I dream of eating them. But I bet they would taste of grit too.

"You could afford *bottled* water if you help me," says Emanuel. "That whole bag full!"

He points to a market girl gliding gracefully towards us along one of the dirt tracks that criss-cross over Trashland. I know her. Her name is Gifty. She's round here most days, selling boiled eggs from a bowl balanced on her head and mineral water from a basket. Gifty is nice, but she takes no nonsense from the guys she passes. Only their money.

As Gifty comes closer, our eyes meet. Her eyes are big and as dark as the smoke clouds blowing about. She looks kind of sad as she tosses me a small bottle from the basket. I catch it automatically.

"Hey," Emanuel calls after her. "How come he gets one for nothing?"

"He's my top student," Gifty says as she walks away. "But he'd better come back to class soon or I won't throw him water. I'll throw him out."

"You go to school?" Emanuel asks me. I can see respect in his eyes.

"It's not real school," I say, shrugging and swigging from the water bottle. "It's at night, in a shack in Old Fadama."

"What is she, fourteen? Fifteen?" says Emanuel. "She's not old enough to be a teacher."

"Well, she is." I scowl. Truth is, Gifty mostly does maths and reading with younger kids. I've not been to her lessons for weeks – I don't like being the oldest there. Anyway, my headaches have been worse, and each lesson costs money. I'd sooner fill my belly than my head.

"Listen, Theo," Emanuel says as he ducks under the sheet back into my tiny chicken shelter. He lowers his voice. "I think we can help each other. I need someone smart who knows his way around."

"Why?" I snap. "What are you on about? Why are you here?"

Emanuel reaches into the back pocket of his shorts and pulls out a handkerchief. He unfolds it. There are lines and words and numbers marked on the white fabric. It's some kind of map.

"I'm here to find treasure," Emanuel says. "Help me find it, and I'll split it with you."

CHAPTER 3

On the Trail

It's a treasure map – and X marks the spot! It's crazy. Like a film.

But this is real life, and right now I have to get to working.

Emanuel says he'll help. Mostly he just stands about telling me his life story while I'm on my knees searching the dirt for bits of metal.

"My older brother used to work in Accra," he says. "He was a smelter in a machine shop.

He melted down scrap metal to make parts for motorbikes ..."

"Did he have his own?" I ask.

"Course. He drove a new motorbike every month," Emanuel brags.

"You're lying," I say. "Smelters don't earn so much." I know cos there are smelters here in Trashland and I hear them bitch about it. They use chemicals on the circuit boards of mobile phones to get at the good metals inside – gold, silver, palladium, tantalum. There's hardly any metal in each phone, so you need a ton of them to make it work. "He must have stolen the bikes," I add.

"Shut up," says Emanuel. "He had lots of money, OK? He was the big man. But something bad happened and he had to leave fast. He hid this treasure so it wouldn't be stolen. He buried it here in this dump and laid low with my aunt and me."

Emanuel draws in a big breath and puffs it back out. "The fumes from the smelting burned out my brother's lungs. He needs doctors. Expensive ones. The treasure he hid can pay for them."

I snort and hold up my magnet. "You think you'll find it with this?"

"I don't know what the treasure is," says Emanuel. His voice is low but intense. "But I'm gonna find it. It's ..." He coughs and wipes his eyes, even though the smoke blowing over the dump isn't so bad right now. "It's my brother's only chance."

"Show me the map again," I say, and hold out my hand. Emanuel checks round to make sure no one is watching.

They're not. Most workers mind their own business, only worrying about their own wallets. But there are some who watch and wait, eyeing your sack. They wait till you've almost filled it, then they beat you up and steal your scrap and sell it to Mr Ghazi.

But Mr Ghazi is pretty good. He listens to us smaller kids when we point fingers at the troublemakers, and he won't deal with thieves once he knows them. But Mr Ghazi won't refund us for any scrap that's stolen. Says he's a businessman, not an idiot.

"It's safe," I tell Emanuel.

He passes me the map. I've been in Trashland so long I should recognise some of it, but I just don't. Why aren't I smarter? I started at Gifty's class to be smarter. I know I can't work the dump for ever – it'll kill me. If I can read and write, maybe I'll get a better job. If I learn maths and numbers, I can make sure Mr Ghazi isn't cheating me. The thought makes me feel strong, even if the sums and reading make my brain hurt.

I don't want Emanuel to take the map to someone who really *is* smarter and split the treasure with them instead.

"I think I know where this is," I tell him.

Emanuel's eyes are hard and bright again. "Show me."

"No! Not now," I say, and shake my head like he's stupid. "You think we can just dig in daylight when anyone can see? The cops will bust us or someone will try to take the treasure off us."

Emanuel swears and takes back the map. "When, then?"

"Maybe tonight. Maybe early tomorrow." I pause. "First you gotta swear you'll split the treasure with me."

"What?" Emanuel says, looking angry. "I told you I'll split it."

"I could tell you I'm the Rock," I say, "it doesn't make it true."

Emanuel stands over me. "The rock's gonna be in your head if you don't show me."

"I want half," I say.

"Half!" Emanuel spits on the ground. "No way. My brother needs that money."

"So you don't have long to get it, do you?" I remind him. "And cos I'm helping you find the treasure and helping you dig it up, I want half."

Emanuel starts swearing again, so I hold up my hands the same way he did to me, telling him, *Be chill.* "You think I'm gonna work for nothing just cos you told me a sad story?" I say. "I got sad stories coming out of my—"

"A quarter," says Emanuel. "I'll give you a quarter of whatever it is."

I stare up at him. I don't even know where this treasure might be, but I know I've got to find out. And I think I know a clever way to do that.

"OK," I say. "A quarter. So long as you shut up now and help me fill this sack."

*

By the end of the day we've collected about four kilos of scrap metal. I take Emanuel with me to see Mr Ghazi so I can get paid. He works out of a shipping container half a mile away across the dump.

Trashland's working day is still in full swing, the different tribes here working to the max. Like they did yesterday, like they will tomorrow. Plumes of thick black smoke blow across the dump to a soundtrack of stuff being smashed.

We pass groups of burners, who torch the plastic covering from wires and cables to get at the copper and aluminium below. The pounders who break up consoles and computers with home-made tools to get at the metals, magnets and machinery inside. And the smelters, like Emanuel's brother, making themselves sick as they strip gold and silver from circuit boards, a few specks at a time.

Mr Ghazi is as big and hard as the chair he sits on. He empties my sack onto the scales. He picks out the bits of stone and dirt that have found their way in. Then he counts out coins for the day's work. It's a few *cedi* – not much in your money, but it'll get me some food.

"Who's this you've brought, Theo?" Mr Ghazi asks. "A new recruit?" He looks closely at Emanuel. "You remind me of someone, son."

"Don't think so," Emanuel says, looking uneasy. "I'm from out of town."

"Oh. Well, every ten years or so I *am* mistaken," jokes Mr Ghazi. His smile doesn't dance with his eyes, though, like it does when he gets money.

"Well, gotta go," I tell Mr Ghazi. "See you tomorrow. Thanks for ripping me off."

It's the same joke I always make, but today Mr Ghazi doesn't bother to pretend he's shocked or check his heart's still beating after my nasty words. He keeps on staring at Emanuel as we go back outside into the stink and smoke.

"That was weird," I say. "Why was he looking at you like that?"

Emanuel shrugs. "He's cuckoo in the head from breathing in burning plastic all day," he suggests. "Come on, man. Show me where my treasure is."

"Not yet," I say. It's time to put my plan into action. "You say you'll give me a quarter of this treasure, yeah? Well, we gotta make it a proper agreement. You have to swear it in front of a witness. Someone responsible."

"Screw that," Emanuel says. "What witness? I don't want anyone else knowing."

"We don't have to say it's treasure we're splitting," I say, and smile. "I know someone."

This is how we end up in Old Fadama that night, looking for Gifty's place.

CHAPTER 4

At Gifty's

Old Fadama is the town that's grown up near Trashland. It's made up of clapboard and breeze blocks and a maze of streets that are more like gutters. A lot of people can't afford the city rents on real houses, so they end up here.

Now and then the government bulldozes some of Old Fadama. But people just pick up the remains and rebuild it. Keep trying. *Yen ko! – Let's go!*

I think it's a good place. They even built some toilets here that anyone can use. I hope Old Fadama is still standing when I have the money to leave Trashland. I want to live here.

We reach the bright blue wooden community centre where Gifty teaches. My plan is to show Gifty the map and see if she can read it. Emanuel will be mad, but I'll tell Gifty it's just a game, not *real* treasure.

I just hope she can figure out where in the dump this treasure was buried.

But Gifty isn't at the community centre. There are families on mattresses here, cooking *waakye* – rice and beans – over a portable stove. Emanuel asks for some. He gets an earful of abuse but nothing for his stomach.

"Gifty lives nearby," I tell him. "We'll find her."

"This is bull," says Emanuel. "I'm getting someone else to help me."

I grab his arm. "Do that and I'll tell everyone what you're doing," I hiss. "You'll get lots more help – they'll dig up the treasure and bury *you* in the hole!"

Emanuel breaks from my grip and pushes me against a wall that creaks under my weight. Someone shouts from the other side. Emanuel lifts his fist like he's going to hit me.

Then we see a kid has come out of the community centre holding a small bowl of *waakye*. She's offering it to Emanuel, looking at him with these big scared eyes.

The family must have changed their minds, and now Emanuel does too. He doesn't hit me. He takes the bowl and scoops out the rice with one hand. I snatch the bowl from him and pick out the last grains. Then I hand it back to the little girl and thank her.

Emanuel gives her a big fake smile and says, "Tell your mum it tasted like crap."

She shrugs and skips off to do just that. Me and Emanuel, we run away fast. We zigzag along the maze of streets, laughing. It's broken the tension between us. And as we catch our breaths, it hits me how lonely I've been. It hits me harder than Emanuel could. Maybe.

Then I hear Gifty's raised voice saying, "I'm not hiding it for you."

"Just a couple of days, Gifty," a man replies.

"No," Gifty snaps. "Not even a couple of minutes."

"We're family!" the man protests.

"I knew there was a reason I don't like you," Gifty spits back. There's a clatter on the steps, and suddenly there she is. Gifty normally looks so cool, but she seems scared and upset

30

now. Her lips are pressed in a tight line. Then she sees me and Emanuel, and it's like she was thirsty and someone threw her water.

"Boys," Gifty cries. "Theo and ...?"

"Emanuel," I tell her.

"Well, it's about time you showed up for your lesson," Gifty goes on. She gives me a look that says, *Back me up.* "It's in my room today, come on. Up the stairs."

Emanuel's already opening his mouth to argue, but he shuts up as a tall skinny man in his twenties skips lightly down the stairs. He has a brown paper package under one arm and his hair is razored. He wears an LA Lakers basketball shirt. He's leaning to one side, like his head's too heavy for his body.

"Hey, boys," the man says. "I'm Gifty's cousin Sammy." When he grins at us, it's like one of the wild dogs in the dump baring its teeth. "She'll be with you just as soon as we sort out our business."

"We have no business," Gifty insists.

"I don't understand how my cousin can teach you anything," Sammy says. "See, she never learns …" He notices Emanuel properly and his face twists into a frown. "Hey. You look familiar."

Emanuel looks away. "Not me. I'm not from round here."

"Wait, I got it," Sammy says, nodding. "He called you Emanuel? You've gotta be Morgan Owusu's kid brother!"

"Nah," Emanuel says. He's looking so scared he must be glad he's standing in the gutter, cos it won't matter if he wets himself. "That's not me."

"You could be twins, man," Sammy goes on, still nodding, still smiling. "It's got to be you. So, is Morgan in town? Sure would like to see him again. I've been worried about his health."

The way Sammy says it puts a chill down me.

"I don't know what you're talking about," says Emanuel. I glance at Gifty and we both know he's totally lying.

Sammy's smile is so wide it's almost splitting his face in two. "Teach this one well, cousin," he says. "Think he needs some wisdom." Then Sammy turns and saunters away. "See ya."

I'm not sure which of us he's talking to.

Pretty soon Sammy's swallowed by the shadows.

"Well," says Gifty. "I don't know what that was about, but you took the heat off me, anyway. Thanks."

"Was that dude right?" I ask Emanuel. "Is Morgan your brother?"

Emanuel nods slowly. "Is your cousin in a gang?" he asks Gifty. "You know. Criminals?"

"Sammy has friends that I don't like much," Gifty says carefully. "But I never met your brother, Emanuel. Maybe he's the exception."

"It didn't sound like Sammy and Morgan were friends to me," I say, and feel a little thrill down my back. If Morgan was in a gang, maybe he really *was* rich and did own all those motorbikes. Maybe this treasure is stolen – then burying it would make sense. Morgan was waiting till the heat was off to collect it.

I suddenly realise that even a quarter of this treasure could really be worth a fortune.

"Anyway, what are you doing in Old Fadama?" Gifty asks.

"We came to see you," I tell her. "We need a witness."

"We don't," Emanuel mutters. But Sammy has scared some of the fight from him.

"Well, come in," Gifty says. She goes up the stairs to the first floor. I pull Emanuel up after her.

I'm impressed that Gifty has a room all of her own. It's small and square. Someone's painted a mural on the wall; I think it's meant to be the Makola food market. Her thin mattress is too big for the room and so the bottom end curls up against the wall. There's a lamp, and a dresser for her clothes, and a hole in the floor where part of a floorboard's been taken out. A hiding place.

I see she has some money tucked inside there. She puts back the floorboard fast and sits cross-legged on it.

"What did Sammy want?" I ask her.

"To hide something," says Gifty. "Don't ask. I don't want to get involved and neither do you." She brightens and adds, "Now, why don't you explain what all this is about?"

"It's about a map," I say. "I want ... um ... a second opinion. Show her, Emanuel."

Slowly, he pulls out the handkerchief and passes it to Gifty.

She studies it. "Where did you get this?"

"Found it," says Emanuel.

"It's just a game," I add.

"Good job," Gifty says with a laugh. "Because if this shows treasure, it's in a bad spot." She taps at the scrap of fabric. "The X here is in line with that old Aoli Tomato Paste sign on Hansen Road."

So that's what the words say! I think, then say quickly, "I thought so too," as Emanuel shoots me a sharp look. "Yeah, that really big sign on the scaffolding. A cute tomato with eyes. Like a landmark."

"So why is that a bad spot for treasure?" Emanuel barks, impatient.

"As more and more waste comes in each year, so the dump gets bigger," Gifty explains. "It spreads out along the lagoon. A couple of years ago, this X would've been on a patch of wasteland on the northern strip. But you can't reach it now. The dump has spread out too far. If there really *is* something there, it's probably sitting under three tons of broken microwaves." Gifty offers the map back to me with a shrug. "Your treasure's become a part of Trashland."

CHAPTER 5

X the Unknown

So early the next morning me and Emanuel are standing where X marks the spot. Well, maybe. It's a pretty big area. We can see the big tomato paste sign in the distance across the street.

Gifty told us that the map says the X is 155 steps south-east from the sign and then 30 steps south when you hit the sandbank. But the area has changed since Morgan made his map. There are fences up and piles of crap everywhere, so it's hard to know where to start digging. We could be way out.

That smiling tomato on the sign looks like it's laughing at us. I want to squash it.

Gifty was wrong about the microwaves at least. This part of Trashland has been taken over by a gang of burners and it's covered in big piles of electronics – everything from stereo systems to air-conditioning units. Some guys are breaking them open and pulling out the coloured spaghetti of cables and wiring. The wires get looped up and hung on the end of a rake, then slung into a fire.

Thick black clouds of stinking smoke billow and blow across the dump like swarms of flies. The smoke actually helps cover up the sharp sewage smell from the lagoon, so maybe it's a blessing. Kind of.

Me and Emanuel, we both have shovels. We borrowed them from Mr Ghazi. I said we wanted to dig a bit deeper for more metal. He didn't even charge us. He just smiled and said he liked to help hardworking businessmen.

Emanuel doesn't give off that hardworking vibe. He's leaning on his shovel and moaning. "We don't stand a chance," he says. "We're never gonna find Morgan's treasure."

"If we can't, then Morgan's screwed," I remind him. "You told me that without being able to pay for doctors he'll die."

Emanuel doesn't answer. I look all around. The cute tomato on the sign stays smiling in the face of that black fog as it gusts across the food market.

I bring out my magnet and say, "We might as well start searching."

"Are you an infant?" Emanuel asks, knocking the magnet out of my hands. "It's no good. That fire there could be burning on top of

it. Or it's under that mountain of broken crap."
He points to the sprawling heap of electronics.

"Fine. You give up then," I say, and pick
up my magnet. "All the more treasure for me
when I find it."

"It's not yours." Emanuel tries to bash away
my magnet again, but I keep a good grip on it.

"Don't be a jackass," I tell him.

Emanuel's looking around as if worried
we're being watched. He was like that all last
night too. He didn't want to talk about the stuff
with Sammy. But he stayed awake like he was
on guard duty. I woke when it was still dark
and saw Emanuel had fallen asleep over the
chicken coop.

"Have you seen Sammy anywhere?" he asks
now. "I thought I saw him earlier."

"No," I say, and glance round automatically. "You think Sammy will come after you to get at Morgan?"

No answer.

"Is that why you were awake last night?" I ask. "Is that why you want to give up – in case it puts Morgan in danger?"

"Sammy's never gonna find Morgan," Emanuel mutters.

"And we'll never find his treasure if we don't even try." I nudge him. "So ... try?"

Emanuel nods reluctantly.

The burners haven't noticed the two of us standing here yet. I try to act like I own the place and swagger to the nearest patch of dirt. I start sweeping the earth with my magnet.

It's a strong magnet, but how deep is Morgan's stuff buried? If I have no luck, I'll dig off the topsoil with my shovel and try again. I try to go slow, hold the magnet loose, ready to react to the tiniest movement.

"*Hey!*"

I jump out of my skin. The burners are looking over.

"What the hell?" one guy shouts at me. "This turf is taken."

"Go home to your mummy," yells another. He throws a rock at me. I jump away and just about avoid it. Another rock sails after it.

"It's no good," Emanuel calls. He's already stalking away.

"We'll be back!" I shout at the guys, but they just laugh. I guess I don't blame them, looking at me trying to act all fierce.

But I'm not giving up. Screw them.

Nothing has ever felt as important as this.

*

It's back to work for me. The old everyday work, filling my sack with tiny bits of metal. But it feels a little harder today, a little more backbreaking. All I can think about is the treasure. I imagine finding a case of brand-new iPhones – real ones, worth a fortune, not fakes like the ones they sell in Tip Toe Alley in town. Or maybe it's a holdall stuffed with banknotes, or jewels or nuggets of gold.

My sack is taking a long, long time to fill.

Emanuel doesn't help. First he says he needs to nap cos he was up half the night. So I let him lie in my space in the shack. When I check in an hour, I find he's gone. All that's left is chickens and Mr Ghazi's shovel.

So that's it. Guess I'll never see Emanuel again.

I spit on the ground. Take a deep breath. Get back to work.

Yen ko. Let's go.

*

It's a slow day. I don't find so much metal cos I can't really focus. The sack's hardly half full as the sun begins its downward slope past the smog.

I carry my sack towards Mr Ghazi's office. All the smoke makes me choke. A goat walks out in front of me, grazing on anything it can find amongst the rubble. I push past it, still thinking of treasure and tactics and how I'll kick Emanuel if I ever see him again.

That's when Gifty storms up to me. No eggs balanced perfectly on her head today. She has the basket full of water, but all she's giving me now is the evil eye.

"Give it back, Theo," Gifty snarls.

I stop and shrug. "What?"

"My savings," she says. "I need my savings. I can't be a teacher if I don't have the money to go to school." She's steaming mad, shouting in my face. "I know you saw the money under the floorboard last night. You took it while I was out!"

"No way!" I shout back.

"Give it to me now and I won't tell the police," Gifty warns me. She grabs me and tries to frisk me, patting at my pockets. "*Where is it?*"

I pull away angrily. The next thing I know, Gifty's grabbed my sack from me. She starts emptying it onto the ground.

"You're crazy!" I yell at her. I'm on my knees, scrabbling at the tiny metallic scraps. "I haven't taken your money. I wouldn't."

"Oh, sure!" Gifty hisses. "Well, what about your friend?"

"Emanuel?" I snort, stuffing the metal back into my sack. "He left this morning. I haven't seen him since."

"Then it's him. Oh, God." Gifty swears and it sounds wrong coming from her lips – she's normally so kind and patient. "To think I was going to warn that little idiot!"

I say, "Warn Emanuel about what?"

And she tells me.

CHAPTER 6

Itching and Scratching

"Sammy came to me again this morning," Gifty explains. "His room's being checked by his probation officer and he needs to hide some dodgy stuff."

I feel my eyes widen. "Drugs?" I ask.

"No." Gifty shakes her head. "Silver, I think. Sammy's gang steal truckloads of mobile-phone waste and cook it up for the precious metals." Gifty pauses, looking serious. "I told him to go to hell again."

"Maybe Sammy took your money?" I say.

But Gifty says no – with her eyes and another shake of the head. "We're family. Even Sammy deals fair with family." She chews her lip for a moment. "I think Sammy asking again about hiding his stuff was just an excuse. He seemed really interested in where he could find Emanuel."

I feel cold despite the sweat on my face. "You didn't tell him, did you?" I ask.

"I said I didn't know," Gifty says. "Cos I don't! And then ... Sammy told me some more about your friend's brother, Morgan."

She hesitates.

"What is it?" I push her.

"Morgan was in Sammy's gang," Gifty explains. "He worked as a smelter in a factory that made car parts, so the gang gave him

51

their stolen mobile phones to cook up for the precious metals inside. Morgan secretly stored the metals in the factory until they had enough to sell on. But he ripped his gang off. He took the gold, silver, palladium and whatever, and told Sammy a rival gang had stolen it. Sammy and his friends hit back at that gang. People got hurt on both sides before they realised Morgan had been lying."

Gifty takes a deep breath.

"Both gangs wanted revenge on Morgan," she finishes. "He had to disappear."

"Two gangs wanting him!" I breathed. "No wonder Morgan left Accra and couldn't come back for his treasure."

"And now Emanuel's gone too," says Gifty. "With my money."

"I don't know how to find him," I tell her. "I'm sorry."

"Yeah," says Gifty, sitting down in the dust. She looks just as broken as everything else in Trashland. "Yeah, I'm sorry too."

I'm still thinking about everything she's told me. "Sammy must know that Emanuel can tell him where Morgan is," I say. "So he'll be trying to get Emanuel, won't he?"

"That's why I wanted to warn him." Gifty nods. "Gangs like to trade stuff. Like, Sammy might agree to leave Emanuel alone if Morgan tells him where the treasure is."

"And if he doesn't …" I draw a line across my throat, like a knife slitting it.

"Sammy wouldn't kill anyone," says Gifty. But she doesn't sound like she's sure.

I imagine Emanuel locked up someplace, tortured into revealing where his brother is. Locked up in the back of a white panel van. Alone and afraid.

But something tells me Emanuel won't need much persuading to spill his brother's secret.

"Screw this," I say, standing up. "I've got to take this scrap to Mr Ghazi before he closes up." I look at Gifty. "You ... can share the money I'll get for it."

She snorts. "Half of nothing is still nothing. Didn't I teach you that already?"

"Fine," I hiss. "Go hungry."

Gifty looks at me, and her eyes soften. "I'm sorry, Theo," she says. "That was kind of you. But you need to eat too."

I turn and leave Gifty there in the dirt. My eyes feel hot as I walk away. The treasure! It's so close I can almost feel it in my hands. I feel bad for still wanting it now Emanuel has gone, but I do.

I know where it is.

The treasure may be stolen, but that was ages ago. No one will be looking for it except criminals.

If I find it, I can sell it fast. Get money.

I would do good things with that money. I could even give some to Gifty, so she will still teach me.

But the treasure is out of reach. I hate that feeling. It's like an itch I can never scratch.

*

There's a line of kids outside Mr Ghazi's cabin, waiting to be paid for the bits of metal they've found. Twenty blank faces waiting for the coins that will fill their slack jaws with food tonight so they have the strength to do it all again tomorrow.

It's only cos I'm at the back of the line that I see where Mr Ghazi is. He's like fifty metres away, talking to some guy on the other side of his cabin. And there's a tall scrawny kid standing between the two of them.

It's Emanuel.

I watch with my breath held as Emanuel hands something to the guy. It's money. I just know it has to be Gifty's cash.

What is happening?

The guy counts the money and nods. He shakes hands with Mr Ghazi. Then the guy turns around and leaves with Emanuel. Mr Ghazi goes back to his cabin. In a second, Emanuel and the guy have disappeared behind a row of filthy tents and fresh gusts of smoke.

"Hey!" I yell. I leave the line without thinking and stumble after Emanuel. *I'm gonna smack him*, I tell myself. He ran out on me.

Stole from Gifty. Made his own plans like I'm nothing.

I'm not nothing.

"Emanuel!" I'm yelling. "Come here, you son of a bitch!"

I reach the row of tents half buried under ash like they're hiding. Looking around, I don't see Emanuel anyplace. I choke on the smoke blowing from across the dump. A fleck of ash gets in my eye. It stings and waters, and I can't see. Where are they?

Wiping my eyes, I stagger forward and almost crash into a group of goats being led by a little kid. I push my way past them and set off across the maze of rusting cars and shipping containers and shacks and shelters.

There's the boom and clash of metal on plastic, telling me this part of Trashland is busy with pounders – the men and women who break apart electricals to get at the stuff inside. They look as worn out as their tools and equipment.

I ask about Emanuel and the guy, but no one has seen anyone come past. I pick a new path and I'm almost crushed by a large truck reversing over the uneven land. Its dented rear door flaps sadly like a broken wing. I scramble up a scrap pile and sit on the side of a half-buried fridge.

No good. I've lost Emanuel and the man with the money.

But Mr Ghazi must know what they're up to!

I race back to Mr Ghazi's office. My thoughts are racing too. Does Mr Ghazi know about the treasure? He gave us the shovels without question ... Was he handing over Emanuel to a gang member cos nothing was dug up? Or was Emanuel paying the guy to get himself safely out of town ...?

The line outside Mr Ghazi's cabin is still long. I take my place at the back of it. The seconds pass slowly to the broken rhythm of the pounders as they work. I'm sweating. Only my mouth is dry. I want answers badly, but maybe I shouldn't say anything to upset Mr Ghazi. He could stop me working here. Then where would I go?

Maybe I should just stay quiet. It's not like I've lost anything real. Not like Gifty. Maybe the treasure isn't my only chance to get out of here?

Or maybe it is.

I wait in line and wonder what I'll do. I feel like one of the chickens in the coop. There's only dirt to eat, but if you don't eat it, you die.

CHAPTER 7

Confrontation

Mr Ghazi looks happy when I finally get inside. He is whistling under his breath.

"Ah, Theo. Last customer of the day. My hardworking hero!" he says, beaming. "Where are my shovels? Not much in your sack. You are losing your touch, perhaps?"

I'm not losing anything else, I tell myself.

So I sling my sack on his desk and the words spit from my mouth: "I saw you with Emanuel, Mr Ghazi."

His smile slips. "You're mistaken, Theo."

"No. I saw." My breathing's so fast it's making me dizzy. I try to slow it down. "Emanuel gave that guy money and when you left, so did they. What's going on?"

Mr Ghazi gets up stiffly and crosses to the door, pulling it shut to dampen the din of the pounders outside. Then he turns and walks towards me. His face is hard, like it's turned to stone. "All I've done for you, and this is how you speak to me?" Mr Ghazi's voice is low and it sounds dangerous. "Who do you think you are, Theo?"

It's like Mr Ghazi's got bigger with the door closed and the world shut out. He's filling the space – if I tried to run now, I'd never get past him.

He leans towards me and says, "I asked you, who the hell do you think you are?"

I want to curl up really small, but something won't bend in my body. I stand my ground and I grit my teeth so they don't chatter. "You call me ... a hero."

Mr Ghazi flinches, just a bit.

"Emanuel is my friend, sir, and I'm scared for him," I say. "Bad people want to get him."

"So I'm bad people now?" Mr Ghazi says. His voice is quieter, but his eyes are like dark spotlights burning into my own. "I try to help others, all my life. Day in, day out in this stinking hole, and this makes me bad?"

"No, sir. Not you." I get the feeling now that it's not really me he's angry with but something bigger. "I think Emanuel is in trouble."

"We are all in trouble, Theo," Mr Ghazi says. Slowly, he straightens again. There's a kind of smile cracking slowly across his stone face.

"So, my little hero. You are worried for your friend, that's all?"

"He stole money from my teacher, Mr Ghazi," I tell him.

"I don't know anything about that," says Mr Ghazi. "This is Trashland. If I spent my days finding out who stole what from whoever …" He laughs gruffly. "The man I introduced to your friend works for Ghana's Green Advocacy group." He sees my face is blank, and so he explains: "This group have scientists who measure the levels of toxic chemicals in the soil here. They have to take samples in a wide area. This man said he can train Emanuel for a job."

I blinked. "He can?"

"But it costs money," Mr Ghazi went on. "Like school costs you money. Emanuel might earn a good wage someday, with the right training."

"Oh ..." I say, and think back over what I saw. Emanuel would have to be an idiot to stick around Trashland. Gifty will get him, or the gangs will.

Or maybe I can get to him first.

Because I think I know what Emanuel is really up to.

There's a loud squeal from the metal door as Mr Ghazi pushes it open. The light outside is dull and grey. "You should hurry along, Theo," Mr Ghazi says. He empties my sack of scrap onto the scales and sighs. Then he reaches into his pocket and drops some *cedis* into my hand. I gasp at how many there are.

"That's more than this scrap is worth," Mr Ghazi says. "But tomorrow I want you working hard all day – so buy something to eat. You're a good kid, Theo. You know I look out for you."

"Thank you, sir," I mumble. What's happening? Is Mr Ghazi trying to say sorry – or trying to shut me up?

"Rest tonight, OK?" he goes on, more like the normal Mr Ghazi, not the scary stone version. "No more dreaming. No more mixing up what's real and what's not." He steers me towards the door. "Looks like it's going to rain hard tonight, Theo. Go straight back to your shelter and stay there."

And it hits me: the way Mr Ghazi's smile broke past his stony face before was like the rumble in the clouds that comes before a storm breaks.

*

Just a few minutes later, the sky is like a grey sponge squeezing its contents out over the world. The rain brings down all the toxins in the air. My head aches and my lungs sting.

Night-time gathers behind the storm clouds, and I sit in my tiny shack beside the chickens. I watch the outside through holes in the sheet. The chickens peck and pace like they're nervous.

I hardly sleep. There's an iron taste in the back of my throat. The rain stops before it's light, and that's when I head out into the dump. My crappy trainers squelch in the slimy mud. A goat sees me from behind a pile of old car exhausts. God knows what it's chewing on.

We all have to survive here however we can.

And like Emanuel, I know that the ground can hide surprises.

The sun's rising as I reach the place where X marks the spot. I see something solid in the shifting shadows.

And then I know I guessed right.

Emanuel is good at changing plans. He thought he could find his treasure in the dirt with a magnet. But he couldn't, so he had to think of something else.

He thought he could dig up the treasure with a shovel. But he couldn't, so he had to think of something else.

So now, here in the shadow-light, is a huge mechanical digger, parked up and ready to swallow down Trashland's bedrock. It looks as if it could tear out the Earth's core.

That's why Emanuel paid Mr Ghazi's friend who works for the Green Advocacy group. They can go anywhere to get samples of Trashland's soil. I've seen these big diggers in action. They dig deep to see how far the pollution has spread. They roll in on anyone's turf. They're allowed to. No one stops them.

But I know that this digger isn't here to collect soil samples.

Today, at last, Morgan's treasure is coming out of the ground.

CHAPTER 8

Lost and Found

I sit on a rock and watch as Trashland slowly comes to life with the new day. People appear from sagging tents and between gaps in plywood. Someone pokes a fire into red flickers. Coils of wet cable are forced into flames that spit and hiss, belching out black smoke.

Then I hear a voice in the distance: "Come on. It has to be early. We don't want too many people seeing." The voice breaks off into fierce coughs.

It's Emanuel. I guess he's talking to the man I saw yesterday – the man he's paying for the digger with Gifty's money.

I hide behind an old oven that's sinking into the ground like a shipwreck. Emanuel comes into sight with Digger Guy. Digger Guy looks rough. He probably spent Gifty's money on a good time last night. Emanuel is pretty much pushing Digger Guy along.

Scowling, I wish I was big like Mr Ghazi so I could loom over Emanuel. *How dare you?* I would say to him. *How dare you take my help and then leave me out of this?*

I watch from behind the rusting oven as Digger Guy climbs into the digger and it chugs into life. In a minute it's munching at the ground like a kid eating chocolate pudding. The digger's engine growls, throwing out smoke. The wisps of black are soon lost in the deeper clouds from the burning wires. Emanuel's coughing as the fumes blow over him – he's

not used to things here. He still looks clean.
Hopeful.

Seeing the hope on his face makes me
so mad.

I realise now that Mr Ghazi must have heard the whispers about the treasure too. Mr Ghazi recognised Emanuel cos he looks like Morgan. I wonder how much his share will be?

Mr Ghazi is a businessman, so he will have got himself a good deal. He's taking no risks – he didn't even pay for the digger; Gifty did. So if the gangs come after Mr Ghazi, wanting their stuff, he can deny he knows anything. I can almost hear him telling Sammy: *The Green Advocates said they were testing the soil. I don't know what they found. Take it up with them!*

I watch as the digger pushes some scrap out of the way. It's carving a trench into the ground. Not too deep, but wide. Emanuel is standing close by – just ten metres from me – watching the ground as it crumbles and shifts. He's tensed and focused. He's ready to stop Digger Guy the second he spots something gleaming.

Some burners come up to Digger Guy, complaining he's on their turf and stopping them from working. Digger Guy pulls a piece of crumpled paper from his pocket and waves it at them. "I have to be here," he says. "Take it up with those do-gooder Green groups, not me!"

The hours pass by, smothered in smoke. I ache all over, crouched here out of sight. I know I should be working, but I have to see this through. I feel my stomach growl and wonder if I'll get any food today.

It gets close to noon. I can see that Emanuel is bored, fidgeting. He's also looking kind of worried, staring about behind him. I guess he thought he'd be rich by now.

The digger moves backwards and forwards. It's making a hell of a mess. You could play five-a-side soccer in the area it's chewed up. And all these dead appliances are being pushed aside, piling up like a wave that's set to crash down on the burners as they go about their business. The digger keeps biting into the toxic soil, hungrier than I am. More and more earth is scooped up and emptied out.

And then Emanuel jumps to his feet and yells at Digger Man to stop.

He's seen something.

It looks like a thick flap of dirty skin. It's a plastic sheet, wrapped around something in the ground to protect it. While Digger Guy backs up, Emanuel jumps into the shallow pit in the soil and starts to pull at the plastic.

"Need a hand?" I call.

Emanuel jumps like he's been hit by lightning. He stares round wildly, sees it's me and looks so busted.

"What are you doing here?" he stammers. "How'd you know?"

I shrug. "I saw you pay this guy. I guessed what you were buying and where you'd dig."

"I was going to tell you," says Emanuel.

"No you weren't," I say, and walk past him, staring at the thick plastic wrap. Whatever's inside, I guess Morgan buried it just beneath the surface. But as time passed and rain kept falling, the soil and sand got mixed about and the treasure has sunk deeper and deeper.

"What have we got?" I say, falling to my knees to get a closer look.

"What have *I* got," Emanuel argues, pushing in beside me. "It's my treasure."

"We had a deal," I remind him.

Emanuel shrugs. "I paid this guy to dig it out."

"With money you stole from Gifty," I say. "Gifty's mad at you. She thinks you've left Accra. But if I tell her you're still here, she will set her cousin on you in a moment."

Emanuel glares at me. "I'm gonna pay her back."

"You better," I tell him. "But not out of my share!" I start tugging at the thick plastic. It's heavy. Emanuel tries to push me away, but I shove him back. My magnet is in my hand and I press it to whatever's under the plastic. I want to say, *See? My magnet found treasure just like you wanted it to. You were right to want my help!*

But the magnet doesn't stick. If it's metal it should stick, right?

Emanuel grabs my wrist and twists. I drop the magnet as he tries to pull me away.

"Hey! Hey!" Digger Man shouts. He's suddenly beside us, pushing us apart. "Let *me* see what this is." He has a knife and slashes at the plastic. It hits something hard beneath. Something real.

Me and Emanuel look at each other. We stop fighting and yank at the cover.

A handlebar points at us like an accusing finger.

We heave and pull at the plastic. I realise my magnet has fallen into the split and now it's clinging to a chrome headlight. I snatch it back as Digger Guy strips away more of the plastic to reveal chipped paintwork on a red front axle. A mudguard. A dead metal body.

"What the hell?" Digger Guy swears as he looks at Emanuel. "This is your big treasure? It's a motorbike, kid. Just an old motorbike!"

CHAPTER 9

Lockup and Breakout

By nightfall the bike is standing in Digger Man's lockup, where he keeps all his tools and stuff. A dim bulb shines over the bike like a cheap spotlight.

We kept on looking for the real treasure all afternoon. A crowd of burners ended up watching us work, asking us stupid questions: *"What are you after?"* *"Don't you have enough dirt yet?"* We ignored them and kept on searching.

But we found nothing more. If there was real treasure here, it must've been dug up and taken by someone long ago.

It was almost night-time when Digger Man announced he was giving up. Emanuel had paid him for a day and that day was done. So we packed up the bike and heaved it onto the digger and drove away, leaving one hell of a crater in the ground behind us. We rumbled past so many tired workers stumbling on their way to grab some rest.

I guess word will spread that we dug something out of the ground.

And that something is a battered old Yamaha YBR125.

We've unwrapped it, cleaned it off a bit. It's an ordinary motorbike. Not even a cool high-speed model.

I'm so gutted. I can't believe what I'm looking at. In my mind we were digging up a treasure chest crammed full of precious metals. Not an old bike. Some parts of it look newly painted, but others are scratched and bare. It's like this bike was a project Morgan started, but it got buried before he could finish it.

Emanuel is staring at the bike like it will change into something new if he wishes hard enough.

"Key's in the ignition," Digger Man says, tapping in front of the handlebars. "It has a single-cylinder engine, air-cooled. Not much to go wrong, even when it's been buried in the ground for years."

Digger Man mounts the motorbike and twists the key. He checks the fuel tap is on and presses on the kick-starter a couple of times to get compression. He gives the throttle a twist and with a firm kick tries to start the engine.

Nothing happens for two more kicks.
Finally, the engine starts, and its throaty roar

bounces around the lockup's rusting metal walls. Smoke from the exhaust stinks up the enclosed space as Digger Man adjusts the rear-view mirrors on their long metal stems.

"Plenty of fuel!" Digger Man yells. "Yep, all good to go!"

"Get off!" Emanuel swats Digger Man's hands from the throttle. "It's not yours."

Digger Man shrugs and switches off the engine. The ticking in the sudden silence is somehow just as noisy as the engine's hungry rumble. "I guess your brother planned to use this for a quick getaway," Digger Man says.

"Then why bury it?" I ask. "Doesn't make sense. You can't go anywhere quickly if you have to dig up your getaway vehicle first."

"Whatever," says Emanuel, inspecting the bike. "This bike has got to be, like, fifteen or twenty years old. How much is it worth?"

Digger Guy looks it up and down like it's an animal at market. "In this state, maybe eight hundred *cedi*. If I do it up well, I might get fifteen hundred *cedi* for it."

It sounds like a fortune to me. But for some people in Accra that's not even a month's salary. This can't be the treasure that Morgan buried. He was marked for death by two gangs for what he stole. Fifteen hundred *cedi* can't be worth a life – can it? My magnet didn't even stick to the handlebars, so the metal must be bad, or else it's plastic or something.

Emanuel starts arguing with Digger Man. "What do you mean, *you* might get fifteen hundred?" he says. "You're not getting anything for it. I paid you to dig it up. Now it's mine."

"You're just a kid!" Digger Man replies. "How will you smarten up this heap to get the best price? How are you gonna sell it to anyone?"

"I'll take care of it," Emanuel insists. "I need that money." He pauses. "My brother's counting on it."

"Yeah. Well," Digger Man says, looking between us. "We should talk to Mr Ghazi about who's counting on the money."

"You talk to him," Emanuel snarls. "I'm taking my brother's bike. I'm done with all this."

"Whoa, chill," I tell Emanuel. "I've got a stake in this too, remember."

Emanuel sneers, "Like hell you do."

"It was me who worked out what the map meant!" I say.

"It was Gifty," he argues.

"I took you to Gifty," I remind him. "You could never have paid this guy if you hadn't stolen from her. You said you'd pay her back and you have to pay me too."

"Boys, boys! Relax," Digger Man says. "You've got nothing to fight about." He smirks at us. "Your bike is in my lockup. That makes it mine." He crosses to the door and opens it. The night outside is as black as burners' smoke. "Now, get out of here. Go on, scram. I need to see Mr Ghazi."

"We're not going," I tell him.

Digger Man grabs me by the arm and Emanuel by the collar and hauls us outside into the stinking darkness. I blink, my eyes trying to adjust.

"Get off!" I shout, and try to squirm free of his grip. "You can't just steal that bike."

"It's stolen already," says Digger Man. "Finders keepers."

"You would never have found it without me!" Emanuel cries.

That's what I tried to tell you, I realise. Did I sound as whining and weak as he does now?

"Let the grown-ups take care of this, OK?" Digger Man says. He pushes us both away and turns his back on us. "Go crawl back down whatever hole you came out of." He's no more than a shadow in the silvery smog of the moonlight. He starts to push shut the door to his lockup, reaching in his pocket for the key.

That's when Emanuel brings down a rock on the back of Digger Man's head. Digger Man's forehead bounces off the corrugated metal door and he sinks to his knees, leaving a dribble of blood smeared on the metal.

My stomach has twisted into a tight knot. Emanuel stands there, panting for breath.

I crouch beside Digger Man in the pale moonlight, searching for the split in his skull. I put a hand on his arm and he falls backward, eyes shut. There's a nasty cut on his forehead as well.

I look up at Emanuel. "He's still breathing," I whisper.

"Pity," says Emanuel. He's trying to sound cocky, but he looks like he wants to be sick. "Come on, Theo. We've got to get the bike away from here."

"Oh, so now it's 'we', huh?" I say. Slowly I stand up, glaring at him. "*Now* you want my help – now you've half-killed this guy and know he'll have the cops on you when he wakes up!"

Emanuel shrugs. "He didn't see who hit him. I'll tell any cops that you did it."

"Me!" I stare at him, outraged.

"You just can't trust him, kid," comes a voice from the darkness. "He lies. He cheats. He squirms. Just like his big brother Morgan."

I feel frozen to the spot as Sammy steps into sight.

Two more big guys are standing behind him. They've got Mr Ghazi, who's hunched up between them. One of his eyes is swollen shut and his nose is bust open. Blood and spit bubble from Mr Ghazi's lips.

"I think it's time we all had a talk," says Sammy, showing us the knife in his hand. "Don't you?"

CHAPTER 10

Things Kick Off

I glance at Emanuel. He doesn't look at me. His eyes are fixed on Sammy's blade, which is made sharper by the moonlight glinting on its silver edge.

"Mr Ghazi told us he'd been helping you boys find Morgan's treasure," says Sammy. "He thought he could sell it back to us. Bless." He turns and rubs Mr Ghazi's head fondly, like Mr Ghazi might rub mine. "He actually thought we would pay him for finding it."

"I'm sorry, Sammy," Mr Ghazi splutters, a thick strand of bloody spit dangling from his mouth. "Take it. For free. I won't tell."

"Course you won't tell," Sammy says. "If you do, you're a dead man." He turns back to Emanuel. "Speaking of dead men, how's your brother, kid? We'd really like you to put us back in touch."

"I can't," says Emanuel. He's screwed up his eyes. He looks like he's going to cry. "I can't put you in touch."

Sammy raises the knife. "Sure you can, kid."

"I *can't*," Emanuel hisses, eyes still shut. "You called it just now. Morgan *is* dead."

No one speaks for a few seconds.

All I can think is, *You said he was sick. You said he needed the money to get better ...*

Sammy snorts and nails Emanuel with a single word: "Liar."

"It was last year," says Emanuel. "Morgan's lungs gave up. He couldn't breathe." The words start to run from him like the snot from his nostrils. "He was hiding out, couldn't go to the doctor. My ma was looking after him – he told her about the treasure. He wanted her to get it … but she didn't want to get mixed up in stuff."

I'm still as a statue, watching Emanuel. He's not lying any more – I know it. What I'm hearing is the truth at last.

"Then my ma died too," Emanuel says, sucking in a breath and then out it shakes. "Last month. I found Morgan's map when I was selling her clothes. I figured I didn't have much to lose, trying to find the treasure myself."

Sammy glances back at his big buddies and smirks. "You got that wrong," he says. "If I can't get satisfaction from Morgan, maybe I'll take it out on you."

"For God's sake," Mr Ghazi says, struggling against his captor. "He's only a child—" He breaks off with a shout as one of Sammy's boys smacks him on his broken nose.

Now Sammy looks at me. "Get the bike, kid," he tells me.

"It's ..." I'm so scared I can hardly speak. "It's not even worth that much."

"I want it," Sammy insists. "So get it."

I look at the door to the lockup, standing ajar. Digger Man is still out of it on the ground. His key hangs from the lock. What if I closed the door, turned the key and threw it into the dirt and darkness where it couldn't be found?

But even as I think it I know I don't dare. I'm no hero.

Mr Ghazi is looking at me. He nods.

I turn, cross to the lockup and heave open the door. The Yamaha stands inside. I grip the handlebars and kick back the stand so I can wheel it forwards. It's so heavy, I nearly drop it.

Emanuel stares at the bike as I slowly wheel it outside. Sammy's smiling, slow and ecstatic. He's got everything now. He's got it all.

Then fierce white lights snap on, blinding me. I let go of the bike as I cover my eyes, and it tumbles to the ground. I hear Sammy and his mates swear and shout as a heavy engine roars into life.

Next thing I know, Digger Man's digger is hurtling forward. It sweeps between Sammy and the guys who've got Mr Ghazi and smashes into a pile of old computer monitors beside the lockup. The digger's headlights dim as it's half-buried in a white plastic avalanche.

Screens and casings clatter down. One hits Sammy on the leg and he shouts out, the sound loud as the engine stalls and dies.

I try to see who's driving. Mr Ghazi is shoved to the ground as Sammy's two buddies pull the driver out, their fists raised and ready to crush him—

Her.

My heart balloons in my chest.

Gifty was driving.

She's trying to protect her face from the guys about to hit her. "Leave me alone!" Gifty yells. "I called 191. Police are coming."

"What the hell are you trying to do?" Sammy says, back up on his feet. He swats his buddies away from his cousin so he can grab her himself. "Have you gone crazy?"

"I didn't know it was you, Sammy," Gifty says. She's wide-eyed and shaking. "I swear. I saw these kids in trouble and I thought ..."

She stops now as the low growl of another engine cuts through the air.

Emanuel is on his brother's bike. While we were all staring at Gifty, he picked it up and got it started. The headlight flickers like it's winking. Now the Yamaha speeds away, shooting past me like a rocket, swerving around the path, leaving us all behind.

"Get after him!" Sammy screams.

He's not talking to me, but I'm already on it. My tattered trainers pound the ground. Emanuel doesn't know the place like I do. He's fast on the bike, but he's taking the main road that the trucks and lorries use for unloading – a road that winds past the endless piles of rubbish. I can take a quicker path.

Climbing up scrapheaps and scrambling down the other side, I reckon I can make it to the main gates out of Trashland before Emanuel does. And then – what? Do I block his way and beg him, *Take me with you, Emanuel*, or do I knock him off and take the Yamaha for myself? Leave this dump and everyone in it behind me?

Panting for breath, I reach the towering, rusty railings of the main gates. They stand wide open. A short dirt track leads on to the main street, busy with traffic as always. Taxis, cars and buses speed along. All with places to go.

Me and Emanuel, we could go places too.

But how long till he takes off again without me?

I think of Mr Ghazi, beaten and bleeding in the dirt. I think of Gifty, looking so terrified.

The two of them are the closest I have to chances to make more of my life. They're not much. But they're real. The treasure isn't.

I wanted a quick way out of poverty. Emanuel's bike isn't even the quickest way out of Trashland.

I hear the thrum of the motorbike as Emanuel comes around the corner. The bike jolts over every pothole as he heads for the exit. He's staring at the dials, focusing, trying to figure out something. He hasn't seen me.

It's my last chance to decide what I'll do.

Then I hear the pound and skitter of feet climbing the scrapheap behind me. Sammy's mates have come the same way as me. I've led them here the fast way.

They'll get Emanuel.

The first of Sammy's mates reaches the top of the heap and scrambles over. It's the one who was holding Mr Ghazi. He hasn't seen me, and as he jumps to the ground, I push him hard. He falls on his face.

Emanuel is slowing down as he nears the gate. The ground is uneven – the bike's harder to control.

I run out into his path. "Faster!" I scream, and point out the second guy climbing down the scrapheap beside us. "Get out of here!"

Emanuel nods, accelerates and nearly runs me down as he shoots past the gates of Trashland. He races along the dirt track to the main road, ready for the real world.

But Sammy's second friend is pelting after him. He's got something gripped in his fist. Looks like a brick. Even as he runs, he throws it with horrible accuracy.

The brick hits Emanuel on the back of the neck and his head jerks back. The front of the Yamaha lifts.

For a second I think that Emanuel is pulling a fantastic wheelie, a final *Screw you!* to his pursuers.

But no. He's falling off the bike.

Emanuel bumps and rolls out into the traffic. A bus is travelling past. The Yamaha smashes against its side and spins away.

Emanuel disappears under the bus's wheels.

CHAPTER 11

Treasure

Time slows as the bus's brakes scream and the cars behind it honk, skidding to a stop.

I run towards the crash scene. I pass the guy who threw the brick. He's running back the other way, shouting to his friend I pushed over. Scared, maybe. He wanted to stop Emanuel, but now ...

I reach the battered bus. There are people swarming round it like ants drawn to sugar, shouting and crying. I see Emanuel lying in the filthy road. One arm is bent all the wrong way and his right leg ...

I think I'm gonna be sick. There's only thick dark mush below the knee.

I turn away, my head pounding with the urgent shouts of the first responders:

"Kid's still alive; it's a miracle."

"Call 193!"

"He needs a tourniquet on that leg."

"Can't wait for an ambulance. I'll take him to hospital."

My stomach is still turning. I can hear sirens as I cross to the bashed-up Yamaha lying twisted at the side of the road. In the shock of Emanuel's accident, no one's even thought about the bike. Another random victim.

I grab the twisted frame and start to drag it back onto the dirt road leading to the dump. The wheel looks like someone's folded it in half, the tyre's rubber torn half away. The axle is crushed, split nearly in two.

That's when I see something. And it makes my heart flip.

I crouch to take a closer look and then straighten up sharply at the sound of sirens. Blue lights flash wildly in the dark as two police cars swing round onto the dirt road leading to the dump. Gifty really did call them.

And once the police cars have vanished, wailing, into Trashland's shadows, I hear her voice: "Theo!" Gifty yells. "Are you all right?" She hurries across the road to me, sees the dead Yamaha. "Oh my God, what happened? Where's Emanuel ...?"

I feel strangely calm as I tell her about the crash and how it happened.

"That explains why Sammy's friends have scurried away like the rats they are," Gifty sneers. "Sammy went with them."

I nod. My eyes are still glued to the crushed axle. "And Mr Ghazi? Is he OK?"

"I think so, now the police are here. But he'll be too scared to squeal on Sammy and won't want to admit he was planning to sell stolen property." Gifty puts her hands to her head and sighs. "What a mess. What an absolute, total mess."

"Look here," I tell her. "Tell me if I'm crazy."

I point to where the chrome paint has scraped away from the crushed axle. Underneath it a deeper colour gleams, a warmer shine.

"What does that look like to you?" I whisper.

She stares and speaks slowly: "It ... looks like ... gold."

"Yeah. But it can't be," I tell her. "Can it?"

"Do you have your magnet?" Gifty holds out her hand as she says it. I pull the magnet from my pocket and give it to her. She places it against the gleaming axle. The magnet doesn't stick.

"See," I say. "It's nothing."

"It's *proof*," she corrects me. "Gold isn't magnetic. Oh my God, Theo. Emanuel's brother melted down the gold – maybe he made it into bike parts?"

I nod slowly. "It's a perfect way to smuggle the gold out of his factory. Emanuel said he was always riding different motorbikes, so no one would notice him bringing out parts ..."

Gifty holds the magnet to different parts of the bike to see if the magnet sticks. My heart is rising up my throat with excitement. The gear lever and brake lever on the handlebars – we scratch the paint with a stone and underneath there's gold. The wing mirror stems are gold too. So are the foot pegs.

"Morgan never meant to make a quick getaway on this," Gifty realises. "This *was* the getaway."

I notice something under one of the bike's cracked side panels and open the clasp. "Gifty, this bike comes with a tool kit! Maybe we can use it to take off the gold parts ..."

I remove the storage pocket and tip the contents onto the ground: pliers, double-ended spanners, spark-plug socket, screwdriver ... But there's something not right. These tools are rough, unfinished.

"I think they're solid silver," Gifty whispers. "Maybe even platinum."

We look at this fortune just lying on the ground.

And I look up at Gifty. And I say, "What do we do now?"

CHAPTER 12

Dreaming

Six months later

It's taken me a long time to learn how to sleep without the chickens close by. I still worry about them. I hope whoever's living in my shack is guarding them as well as I did. Or maybe the chickens have gone now. Maybe the whole shack's been knocked down.

Stuff does happen, doesn't it? And some of it's crazy.

Home now is a room above a shop on Hansen Road, in the middle of the vegetable market maybe a quarter of a mile from the dump. (I was going to say it's just a stone's throw away, but I remember Emanuel that night and ... no. Just no.)

Sometimes, even now, I get off my mattress and sleep on the floor. It feels more natural. And I'm glad for the splits in the plywood walls that let in the light, and the smells of the food market, and the traffic's endless rumble.

Gifty has a way bigger room, just next to mine. She's even got a proper glass window in the wall. But that's cool. She needs the light cos she teaches kids up there most evenings and the electric lamp doesn't work half the time. And that's after she's been to school herself all day, learning more. Gifty doesn't even have time to change out of her school uniform, but she doesn't mind teaching in it. It shows the kids that she really knows stuff.

She knew how to save our butts six months ago, for sure.

The night it happened, Gifty helped me carry the bike back into Trashland. We dumped it right by the main path and put some sacking over it – just one more wreck at the dump.

The bike gave us a whole load of precious metals. Our problem was that we had no way to convert them into cash. But Gifty reckoned Mr Ghazi could think of something. She'd followed me the night before and watched me go after Emanuel and Digger Guy. She wanted to know how Mr Ghazi was involved, so she followed him to his office and overheard him on his phone trying to deal with Sammy. "*I know a guy who'll pay a whole lot for these … 'goods'*," he'd said. "*But I thought it only fair to give you first refusal …*"

Of course, Sammy came after Mr Ghazi and, well, you know the rest. Gifty had heard that her cousin was recruiting "friends" for action at the dump that night, otherwise she would never have guessed the reason and come looking. Who knows what might've happened?

So me and Gifty went back and talked to Mr Ghazi. And Gifty said he could have the bike.

But Mr Ghazi was afraid to touch it cos Sammy would be after it. If Mr Ghazi got rich suddenly, it wouldn't take a genius to work out how. So Gifty said Mr Ghazi could keep it hidden and carry on as normal. He could wait until the heat was off and he thought it was safe, then sell it and keep whatever he got for it.

In return for the bike, Gifty wanted ... investment.

See, Gifty didn't want to live on stolen money. She wanted a proper place to teach, money to afford the books and the uniform and stuff she needed. She wanted people to believe in her.

Pretty soon, Mr Ghazi became one of them.

He's a businessman, so he already had some money, of course. He agreed to pay back the cash Emanuel took from Gifty. And he agreed to stump up six months' rent on a better place for Gifty to live and work while she got herself into school. Of course, Mr Ghazi would make it all back and a ton more once he'd sold on the bike parts. Gifty didn't care about that.

But I cared.

"You're gonna come out of this all right," I said. "What about me?"

"You can stay with me," she said. "That way you'll have a real address, which should help you find better work."

She was right.

I don't use my magnet now. I'm a scrap buyer – I knock on doors around town each day with my trolley, collecting electronics that don't work. Then I sell the stuff on to a big wholesaler. My wages help pay for our food and bills while Gifty is still in school. I've never walked so far in my life, but I don't care. I feel blessed that I can walk at all.

I mean, it's more than Emanuel will ever do.

The hospital had to take off his leg and he needs a stick to get around. He's the worst room-mate. The snoring is bad, but his night terrors are worse. Man, it's tough when those kick off. I jump out of my skin when he starts screaming and thrashing about. I have to hold him down till it passes and tell him he's gonna be all right. Which is easy to say but harder to believe sometimes.

Just like when Gifty tells me I'm a hero for helping Emanuel so much.

It's only right that I look out for him. If we'd never met, I'd still be dying down in Trashland. But Gifty says that if he wants to stay with us, he has to take her classes and educate himself. That's if he ever wants to do something more than beg in the streets.

"I'm broke," Emanuel says one day in class. "I'm always gonna be broke."

I push his arm. "'Money' broke?" I ask him. "Or 'broken inside' broke?"

"You know that everything comes to Trashland broke," says Gifty, looking out of the window. "If it can't be fixed, we have to help turn it into something new."

I join her at the window. I look out at the smoking dump beyond the busy street market – miles and miles of useless scrap, sent here to Ghana from all across the world. And for each thing that's recycled, there are fifty more coming to take its place.

Will things ever change?

Yeah. *I'll* change. As I get older, I'll learn more and get smarter. Get *even* smarter.

No one knows it, but the night it happened I took a solid gold brake lever from Morgan's Yamaha. I got it off with a screwdriver made out of silver. Both of them are hidden in my mattress now, and they must be worth a ton. One day I'll sell them and use the cash to start my own business, just like Gifty. And my business will be about finding ways to make recycling easier ... ways to help this burnt-out old world of ours, somehow.

I mean it.

I'm not just talking trash.

Discovering Trashland

In 2019 I wrote a book called *Tin Boy*, about a boy in Indonesia having to mine tin illegally. The tin is needed because it's used in the circuit boards that power our technology, such as smartphones. But I found myself wondering: What happens to those shiny new devices when they're discarded?

That's when I started to think about this story. While *Tin Boy* looks at what goes into putting gadgets together, *Welcome to Trashland* explores how they are taken apart.

Recycling waste electrical and electronic equipment is a big problem. The word "recycling" makes it sound like we are doing good for the planet, but often the truth is very different. In 2019 alone, less than 20% of e-waste around the world was recycled responsibly. Forty-four million tonnes of it was left to pollute the planet – either buried in the ground, burned or illegally dumped.

Some of this waste ends up in the scrap section of Accra's Agbogbloshie Market in Ghana – or Trashland, as Theo calls it. There are many more Trashlands around the world. It is here that all the fridges, TVs, laptops, car parts and other electronic scrap items end up. As Theo has explained, this "e-waste" is broken up and burned down for spare parts and to recover the valuable metals inside.

In Agbogbloshie, the workers tend to come from poor farming areas of northern Ghana in search of jobs that will help them support their families or put themselves through school. If they have any cash, perhaps they can buy faulty second-hand items in the hope of fixing them to sell for a profit.

If they don't, or are unskilled, chances are they will end up scavenging like Theo or working unsupervised in the burning sites or breakers' yards, trying to earn enough to survive.

It is dangerous even to live in such a toxic area already hit by high levels of pollution in the air, soil and water, let alone to do such punishing work each day.

And yet recycling this waste is vitally important. For too long, the way things work has been: "Take, make, use, throw". To take better care of the world we need a new system: "Reuse, repair and recycle".

If we keep resources in use for as long as possible, we extract more value from them and slow the rate of pollution. The hope is that, in future, places like Trashland will be better organised and more efficient, with workers respected and rewarded for their difficult work. That's what people like Theo will try to bring about.

There's things you can do too. We all like new stuff, but don't upgrade your phone just for the sake of it. If there's a faulty appliance in your home, see if it can be repaired instead of replaced. Certain charities agree to take second-hand electronic goods, where they are either sold on to raise funds, or donated to households or businesses that may be struggling. This way, less electronic waste will be burned or buried.

We need that to happen – before the entire Earth becomes a Trashland.